One fish
two fish
red fish
blue fish

By Dr. Seuss

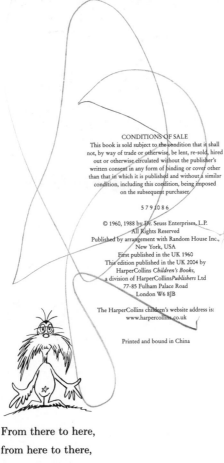

5 7 9 10 8 6

© 1960, 1988 by Dr. Seuss Enterprises, L.P.
All Rights Reserved
Published by arrangement with Random House Inc.,
New York, USA
First published in the UK 1960
This edition published in the UK 2004 by
HarperCollins *Children's Books*,
a division of HarperCollins*Publishers* Ltd
77-85 Fulham Palace Road
London W6 8JB

The HarperCollins children's website address is:
www.harpercollins.co.uk

Printed and bound in China

From there to here,
from here to there,
funny things
are everywhere.

One fish

two fish

red fish

blue fish.

Black fish

blue fish

old fish

new fish.

This one has
a little star.

This one has a little car.
Say! what a lot
of fish there are.

Yes. Some are red. And some are blue.
Some are old. And some are new.

Some are sad.

And some are glad.

And some are very, very bad.

Why are they
sad and glad and bad?
I do not know.
Go ask your dad.

Some are thin.

And some are fat.
The fat one has
a yellow hat.

8

From there to here,
from here to there,
funny things
are everywhere.

Here are some
who like to run.
They run for fun
in the hot, hot sun.

Oh me! Oh my!

Oh me! Oh my!

What a lot

of funny things go by.

Some have two feet
and some have four.
Some have six feet
and some have more.

Where do they come from? I can't say.

But I bet they have come

a long, long way.

We see them come.
We see them go.

Some are fast.

And some are slow.

Some are high.

And some are low.

Not one of them
is like another.
Don't ask us why.
Go ask your mother.

Say!
Look at his fingers!
One, two, three . . .
How many fingers
do I see?

One, two, three, four,
five, six, seven,
eight, nine, ten.
He has eleven!

Eleven!
This is something new.
I wish I had
eleven, too!

Bump!
Bump!
Bump!
Did you ever ride a Wump?
We have a Wump
with just one hump.

But

we know a man

called Mr. Gump.

Mr. Gump has a seven hump Wump.

So . . .

if you like to go Bump! Bump!

just jump on the hump of the Wump of Gump.

Who am I?
My name is Ned.
I do not like
my little bed.

This is no good.
This is not right.
My feet stick out
of bed all night.

And when I pull them in,
Oh, dear!
My head sticks out of bed
up here!

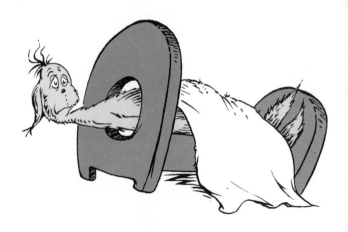

We like our bike.
It is made for three.
Our Mike
sits up in back,
you see.

We like our Mike
and this is why:
Mike does all the work
when the hills get high.

Hello there, Ned.
How do you do?
Tell me, tell me
what is new?
How are things
in your little bed?
What is new?
Please tell me, Ned.

I do not like
this bed at all.
A lot of things
have come to call.
A cow, a dog, a cat, a mouse.
Oh! what a bed! Oh! what a house!

Oh, dear! Oh, dear!
I can not hear.
Will you please
come over near?
Will you please look in my ear?
There must be something there, I fear.

Say, look!

A bird was in your ear.

But he is out. So have no fear.

Again your ear can hear, my dear.

My hat is old.
My teeth are gold.

I have a bird
I like to hold.

My shoe is off.
My foot is cold.

My shoe is off.
My foot is cold.

I have a bird
I like to hold.

My hat is old.
My teeth are gold.

And now
my story
is all told.

We took a look.
We saw a Nook.
On his head
he had a hook.
On his hook
he had a book.
On his book
was "How to Cook."

We saw him sit
and try to cook.
He took a look
at the book on the hook.

But a Nook can't read,
so a Nook can't cook.
SO . . .
what good to a Nook
is a hook cook book?

31

The moon was out
and we saw some sheep.
We saw some sheep
take a walk in their sleep.

By the light of the moon,
by the light of a star,
they walked all night
from near to far.

I would never walk.
I would take a car.

I do not like
this one so well.
All he does
is yell, yell, yell.
I will not have this one about.
When he comes in
I put him out.

This one is
quiet as a mouse.
I like to have him
in the house.

At our house
we open cans.
We have to open
many cans.
And that is why
we have a Zans.

A Zans for cans
is very good.
Have you a Zans for cans?
You should.

I like to box.
How I like to box!
So, every day,
I box a Gox.

In yellow socks
I box my Gox.
I box in yellow
Gox box socks.

It is fun to sing
if you sing with a Ying.
My Ying can sing
like anything.

I sing high
and my Ying sings low,
and we are not too bad,
you know.

This one,
I think,
is called
a Yink.

He likes to wink,

he likes to drink.

He likes to drink, and drink, and drink.
The thing he likes to drink
is ink.
The ink he likes to drink is pink.
He likes to wink and drink pink ink.

SO . . .
if you have a lot of ink,
then you should get
a Yink, I think.

Hop! Hop! Hop!
I am a Yop.
All I like to do is hop
from finger top
to finger top.

I hop from left to right
and then . . .
Hop! Hop!
I hop right back again.

I like to hop
all day and night
from right to left
and left to right.

Why do I like to
hop, hop, hop?
I do not know.
Go ask your Pop.

45

Brush! Brush!
Brush! Brush!

Comb! Comb!
Comb! Comb!

Blue hair
is fun
to brush and comb.

All girls who like
to brush and comb
should have a pet
like this at home.

Who is this pet?
Say!
He is wet.

You never yet
met a pet,
I bet,
as wet as they let
this wet pet get.

Did you ever
fly a kite
in bed?

Did you ever walk
with ten cats
on your head?

Did you ever milk
this kind of cow?
Well, we can do it.
We know how.

If you never did,
you should.
These things are fun
and fun is good.

51

Hello!
Hello!
Are you there?
Hello!
I called you up
to say hello.
I said hello.
Can you hear me, Joe?

Oh, no.

I can not hear your call.

I can not hear your call at all.

This is not good

and I know why.

A mouse has cut the wire.

Good-bye!

From near to far
from here to there,
funny things are everywhere.

These yellow pets
are called the Zeds.
They have one hair
up on their heads.
Their hair grows fast . . .
so fast, they say,
they need a hair cut
every day.

Who am I?

My name is Ish.

On my hand I have a dish.

I have this dish
to help me wish.

When I wish to make a wish
I wave my hand with a big swish swish.
Then I say, "I wish for fish!"
And I get fish right on my dish.

SWISH

ISH

So . . .

if you wish to wish a wish,
you may swish for fish
with my Ish wish dish.

At our house
we play out back.
We play a game
called Ring the Gack.

Would you like to play this game?
Come down!
We have the only
Gack in town.

Look what we found
in the park
in the dark.
We will take him home.
We will call him Clark.

He will live at our house.
He will grow and grow.
Will our mother like this?
We don't know.

And now
good night.
It is time to sleep.
So we will sleep
with our pet Zeep.

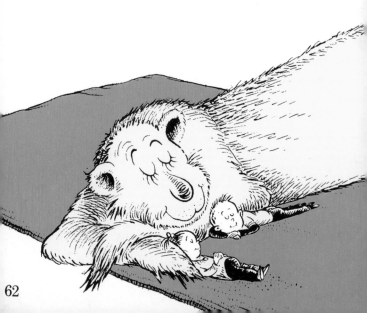

Today is gone. Today was fun.
Tomorrow is another one.
Every day,
from here to there,
funny things are everywhere.

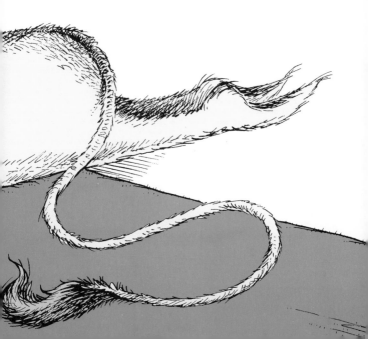